HELLO

LOST

This book belongs to

....

I Spy with My Little Eye

UNICORN WISH & FIND

cottage door press®

Written by Rubie Crowe
Illustrated by Giorgia Broseghini

LOST

Is there something that I'm missing?
What could it be — *of course!*
I'm a unicorn who's lost her horn.
Without it I'm just a horse!

They love it when it's
warm and sunny.
Can you spot 3 happy bunnies?

Can you spot 3 unicorns
with purple horns?

"Can you help me find my horn?
I'll use its magic to grant you a wish."

I spy a ladybug
in a boat.
Will she sink?
Will she float?

Can you count 6 pink flowers?

It's usually so attached to me.
How did it get away?
Let me trace my hoofprints back
through my busy day ...

The unicorn lost
something else, too.
Look in each scene for
a pink horseshoe!

Did it fall off jousting narwhals
in the tournament at sea?

Hey, this is pretty neat!
Can you spot the fish
with a ringside seat?

She thought this was
a masquerade!
Do you see the narwhal
dressed like a mermaid?

That's a silly sight! Find 2 penguins having a splash fight!

WINarwhal WIN

UNICORN GoGo

Can you count 5 blue flags?

Is there a Lost and Found? I found a hat, scarf, and mittens on the ground. Can you spot them?

Perhaps a mermaid found it and is saving it for me.

Did I drop it popping bubbles with the goblins in the bog?

Can you spot 7 slimy frogs?

Can you spot 4 slithering snakes?

SALTS

I spy a unicorn convinced that if she smooches a frog he'll turn into a prince.

POP

This goblin doesn't want to play — find someone enjoying a relaxing spa day.

I spy someone catching a ride. Can you spot a bubble with a beetle inside?

And it's drifting through the swamplands on a mossy floating log?

What's that flying overhead? Can you find a hot-air balloon that's red?

You don't need to be a super sleuth to spot the Tooth Fairy. (Her hat is a tooth.)

I played ring toss with the fairies at their palace in the air.

Someone's napping
in a flower bed.
Can you find them?

Can you find a
yellow fairy hiding
someplace fun?

Can you count 5
orange butterflies?

They take games very seriously.
Perhaps I lost it there?

"I'm trying to paddle this canoe, but I can't find my other oar. Can you?"

This little scout is being very naughty. He's playing a prank on his friend. Do you see?

Can you spot some binoculars?

Picking rubies is quite a project! Can you spy 3 that haven't ripened yet? (They're green.)

I spy a unicorn who
isn't having any luck
setting up his tent.
Now I think he's stuck!

Or maybe my poor golden horn got stuck inside a tree
when I was picking rubies with Sasquatch Scout Troop 3.

Other things can be itchy, too—like woolly sweaters! Can you count 2?

Can you find 5 rakes?

He's got some amazing skills. Can you spot the porcupine with quills?

SCRATCH *line* STARTS HERE

3 bighorn sheep wonder what's the fuss— "Can you save some of those scratches for us!?"

Can you spot 3 helpful raccoons?

I also volunteer on Tuesdays with a group that does outreach,

helping giants scratch their itches
in the spots that they can't reach.

I spy something quite eye-catching:
2 tigers with great claws
for scratching!
Can you spot them, too?

I was locksmith for a worried gnome
who had lost her only key.

Do you see the gnome
who slipped on a slimy trail?

Back of the Yard
BAKERY

Can you find the
gnome in the shower?
(He's been in there
for half an hour!)

Can you count 3 bird houses?

Can you find 5 golden keys?

REDHATShoppe

I'm cooking soup, nice and hot. Can you spy me stirring my big pot?

If anyone could unlock her door, I knew that it'd be me!

I toasted marshmallows with dragons
which was really lots of fun,

UNICORNZ
RULE

Can you
find the bat
wearing a hat?

Can you find 2 dragons
who made a unicorn shadow?
How'd they do it?
I don't know!

Can you count
6 flaming
torches?

marsh
mallows

even though most of our efforts
turned out kind of overdone.

You found the
treasure! Can
you find 8 golden
coins around?

"Hey! Who
threw that?"

"Ye who removes this sword
shall claim the throne."
Can you spot the sword
in the stone?

The kitchen cats love to hide. Can you spy 7 of them inside?

Whoops! Can you find someone clumsy that spilled the flour?

I was with the kitchen witches a little later in the day

"Sugar sparkles and rainbow twinkles ..." Who's casting a delicious spell for sprinkles?

Can you spot 3 broomsticks?

Can you count 5 candles burning?

and we made dozens of donuts in flavors quite gourmet.

I used my horn to play tic-tac-toe with the trolls under the bridge.

Can you spot the troll who's on a roll?

TROLLS ONLY

I spy a goat who's looking gruff. Careful, trolls! Things might get rough!

I never won a single game,
but they do cheat just a smidge.

Winning this game
might be hard.
Can you find the troll
cheating at cards?

Can you count
6 lazy lizards
lounging around?

Can you spot
some sunglasses?

Are there other types
of horns you know?
Some horns play
music when you blow.
Can you find 2?

Can you find 2 insects
dancing? Can you spot
a reindeer prancing?

Sap
Tap

I definitely used it to hang
strings of twinkle lights,

I spy a woodland sprite who is feeling kind of sleepy. Good night!

Can you count 8 glowing lanterns?

Can you spot someone playing pin the horn on the unicorn?

helping decorate the forest
with my friends the woodland sprites.

How could I lose something that was growing on my head?

I go nuts for donuts! Can you find 4?

Can you spot the sword from the stone?

marsh mallows

Can you find a flowery crown? Can you count 8 rubies around?

Can you count 6 magic wands?

LOST

Can you find the pillow that matches this one?

Can you spy a frog who has left the bog?

Can it really be? Oh silly me!
It was underneath my bed!

Did you find the
pink horseshoe in
every scene?
Now look around,
can you count 13?

I spy 2 frogs
and an orange cat
and a penguin in a winter hat.
Can you find them, too?